Written by Philippa Moyle
Designed by Louise Morley

First edition for the United States, the Philippines, and Puerto Rico,
published 1997 by Barron's Educational Series, Inc.

Text © HarperCollins Publishers Ltd 1996
Illustrations © HarperCollins Publishers Ltd 1996
Published by arrangement with HarperCollins Publishers Ltd

The author/illustrator asserts the moral right to be
identified as the author/illustrator of this work.

Illustrations: Charlotte Hard
Photographs:Ardea: 24, /L Bomford 25, /P Morris 26; Bruce
Coleman Ltd: /F Labhardt 8, 24 /H Reinhard 49, /H Rivarola 58b,
/F Sauer 20b, /K Taylor 38b; NHPA: /A.N.T. 4, 15, /A Bannister 9br,
14b, 16, 21, 29, 36, 38, 45, 54, 55, /G Bernard 41, /N Callow 9t, 57t, 58t,
/L Campbell 57b, /S Dalton 12, 13, 17, 19, 25, 26, 30t, 32, 33, 35, 37, 42,
43, 48, 56, 59, /R Erwin 31, /D Heuclin 40, 46, 53, /M Garwood 34,
/P Petit 52, /R Planck 20t, /C Ratier 55 (inset), /K Schafer 44, /J Shaw
22, /E Soder 10, /K Switak 9cl, 30b, /R Thompson 23, /M Tweedie 31;
Natural History Museum: 14t; Natural Science Photos: /J Haas 51b,
/I Lane 51t, /P & S Ward 9bl; Oxford Scientific Films: /G I Bernard 18,
/D Fox 50, /J Mitchell 39, /T Shepherd 27, /D Thompson 9cr.

All rights reserved. No part of this book may be
reproduced in any form, by photostat, microfilm,
xerography, or any other means, or incorporated into
any information retrieval system, electronic or mechanical,
without the written permission of the copyright owner.

All inquiries should be addressed to:
Barron's Educational Series, Inc.
250 Wireless Boulevard
Hauppauge, New York 11788

ISBN 0-7641-5039-1

Library of Congress Catalog Card Number: 97-70524

Printed in Hong Kong
987654321

Minibeasts

CONTENTS

Minibeast Who's Who 8

Ant 10

Bee 12

Beetle 14

Butterfly 16

Caddis Fly 18

Caterpillar 20

Dragonfly 22

Earthworm 24

Earwig 26

Firefly 28

Flea, Tick, and Mite 30

Housefly and Hover Fly 32

Ladybug 34

Locust and Grasshopper 36
Millipede and Centipede 38
Mosquito 40
Moth 42
Praying Mantis 44
Scorpion 46
Snail and Slug 48
Spider 50
Stick and Leaf Insects 52
Termite 54
Wasp 56
Wood Louse 58
Index 60

MINIBEAST WHO'S WHO

The minibeasts in this book belong to six different groups of animals. They are all called invertebrates because none of them has a backbone. On this page you can see one example from each of the six groups. You can find out where all the other minibeasts belong on pages 60 to 61.

A wood louse is a crustacean.

A butterfly is an insect.

A mite is an arachnid.

An earthworm is a worm.

A snail is a mollusk.

A millipede is a myriapod.

ANT

Ants are known as social insects because they live together in nests. Each nest contains a queen, whose job it is to lay eggs, and worker ants who have many different jobs. These involve finding food, looking after the queen,

A leaf-cutting ant carrying part of a leaf back to the nest

Worker red ants looking after the larvae

eggs, and larvae, and guarding the nest. Inside the nests of leaf-cutting ants there are strange fungus gardens. The ants collect leaves and flowers, shred them up, chew them into a pulp, and place them in the garden. The fungus that grows in the garden is eaten by the ants.

BEE

Bees are flying insects that feed on nectar and pollen found in flowers. Some bees live alone but others live together, forming a swarm. A swarm of bees consists of one

A bumblebee searching for nectar and pollen

queen, who lays eggs, and many workers. Bees make honey from the nectar, which they store in honeycombs. The honeycombs are built by the worker bees and have rows of six-sided cells, usually made from wax. Baby bees, called larvae, hatch from their eggs inside the cells. The workers feed the larvae on honey and pollen until they grow into adult bees and are able to collect their own food from flowers.

Worker bees making honeycombs

BEETLE

Beetles come in all sizes! Some of them are tiny, measuring less than .02 in. (0.5 mm) while others, such as hercules, measure more than 6 in. (15 cm). Whatever their size, all beetles have mouthparts that bite and a tough case to protect their wings.

A goliath beetle

Dung beetles in action

Beetles feed on different foods and collect it in different ways. Dung beetles store their food by making large balls of dung, rolling them away, and burying them for later!

A bright jewel beetle resting on a leaf

BUTTERFLY

Butterflies are flying insects with large wings that are usually very colorful. During the daytime they flutter around flowers looking for nectar. They have a long, coiled mouthpart that they uncoil into the center of the

A butterfly at rest with its wings closed

A monarch butterfly in full flight

flower to suck up the nectar. Butterflies rest with their wings touching each other. Butterfly larvae are ugly-looking grubs, called caterpillars. You can find out about caterpillars, and how they become beautiful butterflies, on pages 20 and 21.

CADDIS FLY

Adult caddis flies look something like moths but their wings are covered with long hairs. They are usually found near streams and ponds. The larvae live in water where they build casings to protect themselves. Some of these casings are long, thin tubes, coated with sand. Others are shorter

An adult caddis fly resting on a twig

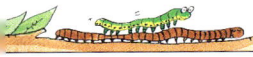

and messier. They are made from small stones, pieces of wood, and tiny shells that are joined together. The casings act as camouflage for the larvae. The camouflage helps the larvae to blend into their surroundings so other creatures will not notice them and eat them.

Above: A messy, pebbly larva casing

Below: A long, thin, sandy larva casing

CATERPILLAR

A monarch caterpillar

Caterpillars are the larvae of butterflies (see pages 16 to 17). They come in many different colors. Some of them are even covered with long hairs. Caterpillars hatch from eggs laid by the adult female butterfly. Young caterpillars spend most of their time feeding so that they develop into a fat chrysalis. Inside the case of the chrysalis, the caterpillar slowly

A very hairy caterpillar!

A citrus swallowtail caterpillar attached to a branch by a tiny silk thread

changes into a butterfly. This change is called *metamorphosis.* When the chrysalis splits open, the adult butterfly appears and flies away.

DRAGONFLY

Dragonflies are colorful insects. Young dragonflies are called nymphs and live in water. They grow into adults in stages by molting.

A shimmering dragonfly

Dragonfly nymphs spend most of their time eating; this one is feeding on some pondweed.

The nymph grows a new stretchy skin under its hard outer shell. Eventually, the hard shell splits away, leaving the new stretchy skin that soon becomes hard. The nymph grows until it fills this new shell and then molts again. The nymph molts many times before it becomes an adult.

EARTHWORM

A wriggling earthworm

Earthworms have a long, thin body, divided into segments, which allows them to wriggle easily through the soil. The segments have tiny hairs that the earthworms use to grip the soil as they move. Although they do not have eyes, earthworms use a special layer in their skin to tell whether it is light or dark. They use their sucking

mouths to eat leaves and bits of rotting plants. Earthworms spend much of their time burrowing through the soil, carrying their food with them. Gardeners are very fond of worms because they help to make the soil more fertile by leaving behind pieces of leaves as they burrow. They also allow air to enter the soil.

EARWIG

Earwigs are insects that live in damp places, such as under the bark of rotting logs. They have a pair of pincers at the front of their bodies that they use to defend

An earwig exploring a flower

A female earwig looking after her eggs and babies

themselves from attackers and to hold their food when they catch it. Earwigs can also use their pincers to make a signal for attracting a mate. Some species of earwigs look after their eggs and the young nymphs when they hatch. Like dragonflies, earwig nymphs grow into adults in stages by molting.

FIREFLY

Fireflies are actually flying beetles. They rest on plants during the day but at night they glow with a greenish light as they fly. Their lights are used as signals; the male firefly sends a flash of light from a special part of his body and the female responds with her own flash of light. Fireflies live mainly in tropical countries and a group of fireflies together can create a stunning fireworks display! Firefly larvae, called glowworms, also send out flashes of light. The larvae hunt down slugs and snails to eat, while the adults feed on nectar.

A glow-worm sending out a flash of light

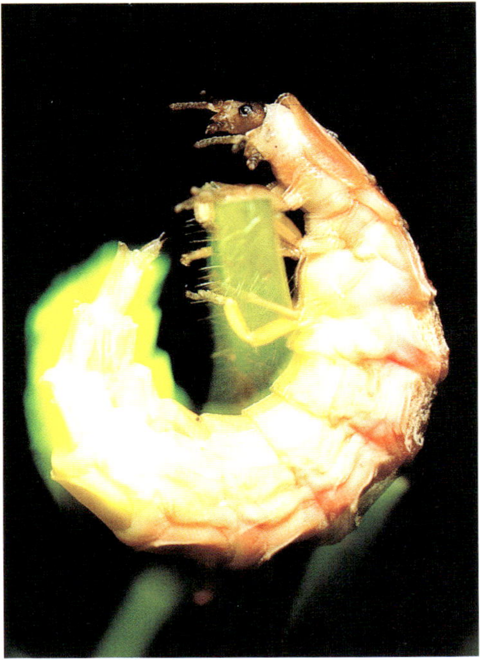

FLEA, TICK, AND MITE

A cat flea leaping

A red mite

Fleas have piercing mouthparts that they use to feed on another creature's blood. They can jump as far as 100 times their size using their strong back legs and are very hard to catch!

Ticks and mites also feed on liquids but their food includes sap from plants as well as blood. Most of them are tiny – adult ticks can be 0.2 in. (6 mm) long but adult mites are often shorter than 0.04 in. (1 mm). Fleas, ticks, and mites can carry disease from one creature to another.

A greatly magnified wood tick!

HOUSEFLY AND HOVER FLY

Houseflies are insects that can carry disease on their feet. They often land on food prepared for people to eat and feed on it themselves. They feed by putting saliva on the food

A housefly on a slice of bacon

and then sucking the sticky mixture into their mouth with a special "tongue." The female fly often lays her eggs in dung and the larvae that hatch are called maggots. Hover flies feed on flowers. They are usually brightly colored because they pretend to be dangerous insects

A hover fly taking off from a flower

like bees and wasps. They are very good fliers, as they can hover in one place and even fly backwards!

LADYBUG

A ladybug on foot!

Ladybugs are brightly colored beetles that are often found in gardens. Their wings are protected by colorful wing cases. Bright red wing cases with black spots are the most common but they can also be yellow, white, or black. Ladybug larvae look very different and become adults through metamorphosis (see pages 20 to 21). Both the adults and larvae feed on tiny aphids that are found on many plants in great numbers.

A ladybug taking off from a flower; you can see its wing case lifted up and the wings behind.

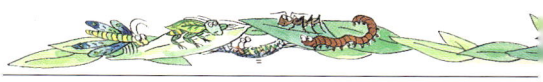

LOCUST AND GRASSHOPPER

There are over 5,000 different kinds of locusts. The biggest locusts have a wingspan of over 6 in. (15 cm) while the tiny pygmy locust is only about 0.4 in. (1 cm) long. Locusts sometimes travel and feed in huge swarms and can cause a great deal of damage to crops. Like locusts, grasshoppers are insects with long

This locust oozes a stinging foam if it is handled.

A meadow grasshopper

back legs that allow them to jump high into the air. Grasshoppers live on the ground and attract a mate by "singing." They make a chirruping sound by rubbing their wings against their legs.

MILLIPEDE AND CENTIPEDE

A millipede curled into a ball

Millipedes have long bodies divided into segments. Most segments have two pairs of legs. Some millipedes have as many as 180 segments (which would give them 720 legs), but about 100 legs is more common. Others have as few as 12 segments and can roll into a ball. Millipedes move one leg after the other so it is not

A millipede on the move

surprising they get around fairly slowly! Centipedes also have long bodies of about 15 segments. They like damp, dark places and you may find them under bark or logs. The giant centipede is about 12 inches (30 cm) long and lives on a diet of insects and mice.

A giant centipede

MOSQUITO

Mosquitoes are insects that bite! They have long, thin mouthparts that make a hollow needle. They use this to pierce the skin of other animals and suck up blood. Usually, it is the females who suck blood, while the males feed on nectar from flowers. Mosquitoes are found all

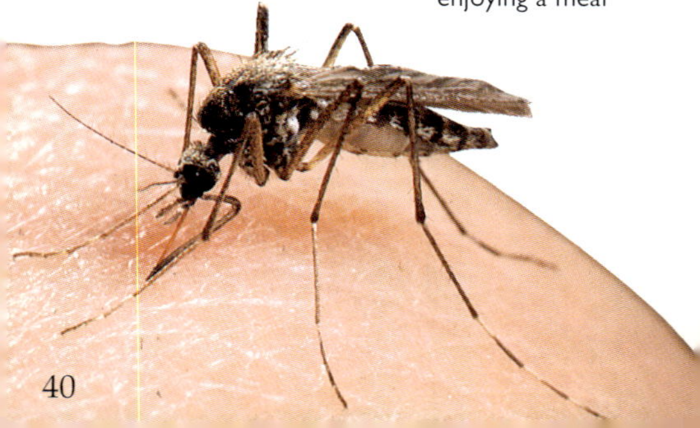

A mosquito enjoying a meal

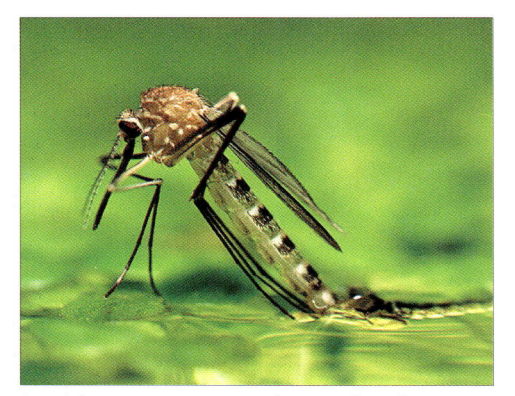

An adult mosquito emerging from its chrysalis

over the world but are particularly common in the tropics where they can carry diseases from one person to another. The larvae live in water and become adults through metamorphosis (see pages 20 to 21).

MOTH

Moths have feathery feelers called antennae.

A scarlet windowed moth camouflaged against fall leaves

Moths, like butterflies, are flying insects with large wings that can be very colorful. Unlike butterflies, moths fly mostly at night. They use a long, coiled mouthpart to suck up nectar. Their larvae are called caterpillars and become adults through metamorphosis

A Rothschild's silk moth

(see pages 20 to 21). The larvae of silk moths, called silkworms, are important for producing silk fabric. The silkworms spin silken cocoons around themselves that are collected, made into silk thread, and woven into fabric.

PRAYING MANTIS

It is easy to see why praying mantises were given their name.

Praying mantises are mainly tropical insects. They have spiny front legs that they flick out to grab their prey and hold onto it tightly. They are colored to blend in with their surroundings. Some mantises are green or brown to look like living or dead leaves. Others are the color of a particular flower. When they hide on these flowers, they seem to disappear from sight!

This mantis looks like a beautiful pink flower.

44

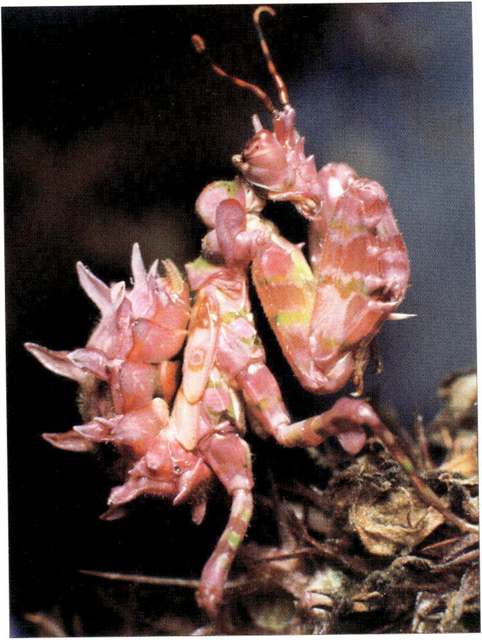

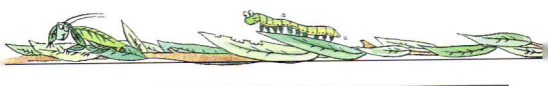

SCORPION

Scorpions are well known for their sting, located at the rear end of their body. At the front end is a large pair of pincers. Scorpions mostly sit and wait for their prey to move fairly close to them and then grab it with their pincers and inject a sting that prevents the prey from moving. Scorpions usually hide under logs or stones during the day and become active at night. They are found in most warm countries and in hot places such as deserts.

Fat-tailed scorpions showing their long tails and stings

SNAIL AND SLUG

A red slug

Snails range in size from tiny water snails to the generally larger land snails. They have a hard shell coiled in the shape of a spiral that varies in color and pattern. If a snail is frightened it can hide inside its shell for safety. It pulls itself into its shell, head first. Young snails look like tiny adults. As they grow, more coils are added to their shells. Slugs usually do not have a shell.

Snails and slugs move along the ground on the flat underside of their body, which is called a foot. Snails and slugs sometimes ooze a slimy substance from their bodies to help them glide along more smoothly.

A dark-lipped banded snail on the move

SPIDER

The hairy body and legs of a large tarantula can seem threatening.

Spiders vary greatly in size from tiny, harmless ones to huge, hairy tarantulas famous for their bite! Spiders mostly feed on insects and have developed amazing methods of catching their prey. The most common is to build a web of silk threads. *Orb* webs catch flying insects while *sheet* webs trap crawling ones. Jumping spiders surprise their prey by leaping on it from a distance, while crab spiders hide in flowers and wait for insects.

A garden spider

A spider mending its web

STICK AND LEAF INSECTS

A female stick insect

As their names suggest, stick and leaf insects look just like sticks and leaves! Stick insects are long and thin to look like the twigs and plants they feed on. They are some of the biggest insects, as they can grow to over 12 in. (30 cm) in length.

Leaf insects live in tropical climates. They have stubby bodies and legs with flattened parts attached to them. These help the insects to look like part of the plants they feed on. Some look like fresh green leaves while others have "dead" brown and yellow patches.

This leaf insect looks as if something has been nibbling on it!

TERMITE

A queen termite

Termites are social insects found in the tropics and North America. The nests of some species are huge mounds made from soil particles mixed with the termites' saliva. Soldier termites guard the nest. Inside the nest is a maze of passages and chambers – nurseries for the larvae, gardens for growing food, and the royal cell where the king and queen termites live. The queen's body contains thousands of eggs.

A huge termite nest; the inset shows winged termites.

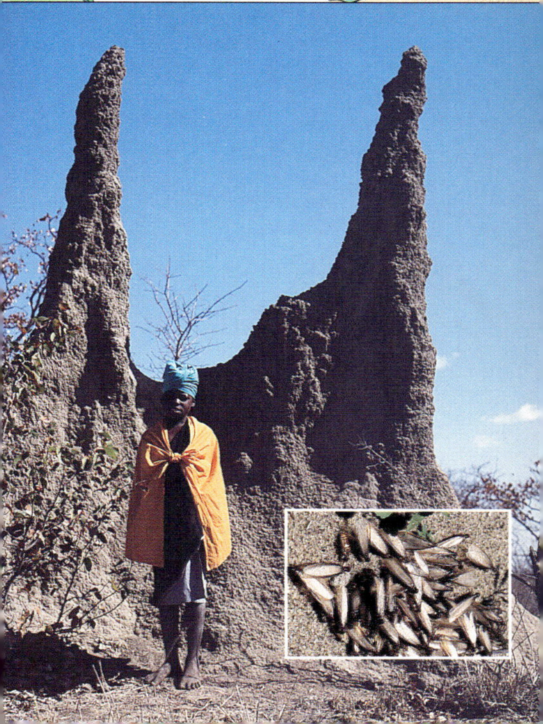

WASP

Wasps are flying insects well known for their sting. Some species of wasp live alone, while others are social, living together in large nests. Many wasps build their nests in trees; others attach them to buildings.

A gall wasp hanging from a branch

A paper wasp setting off on another journey

A common wasp worker

There are even some underground nests. The workers make the nests from wood that they chew to produce a pulp. Paper wasps nibble this pulp into a thread of paper with which they build the nest in layers. Gall wasps live alone and feed on plants where they lay their eggs. As the larvae grow, the plant forms round galls around them that protect the young wasps.

WOOD LOUSE

A wood louse molting

A pair of pill wood lice

Wood lice are crustaceans and are related to crabs and shrimp. Most crustaceans live in the sea but wood lice have adapted to life on land. They have flattened bodies made of segments, and seven pairs of legs. As their name suggests, they live in woodland and hunt for food among the fallen leaves, twigs, and logs. They have strong mouthparts that they use to bite and chew food. Wood lice lose water from their bodies in dry air, so they are active mostly at night when the air is damp. Young wood lice look like tiny adults and develop into them by molting (see pages 22 to 23).

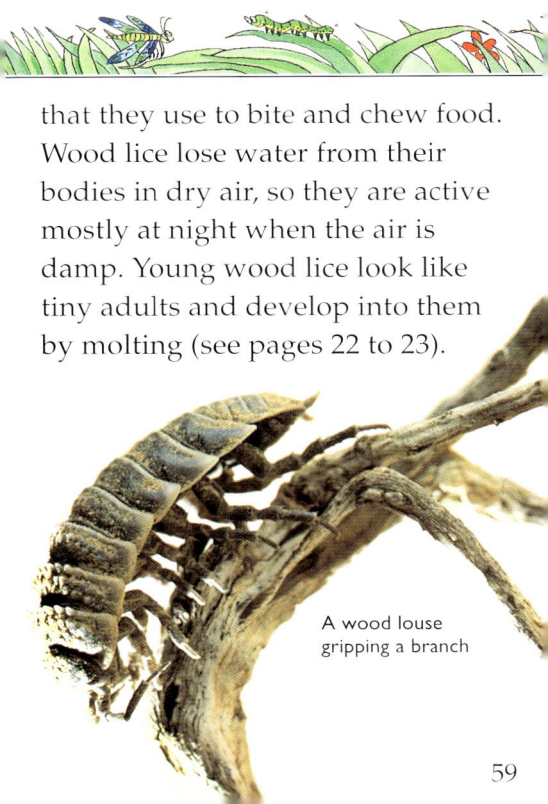

A wood louse gripping a branch

INDEX

ARACHNIDS
Mite 30–31
Scorpion 46–47
Spider 50–51
Tick 30–31

CRUSTACEANS
Wood louse 58–59

INSECTS
Ant 10–11
Bee 12–13
Beetle 14–15
Butterfly 16–17
Caddis fly 18–19
Caterpillar 20–21
Dragonfly 22–23
Earwig 26–27
Firefly 28–29
Flea 30–31
Grasshopper 36–37
Housefly 32–33

Hover fly 32–33
Ladybug 34–35
Leaf insect 52–53
Locust 36–37
Mosquito 40–41
Moth 42–43
Praying mantis 44–45
Stick insect 52–53
Termite 54–55
Wasp 56–57

MOLLUSKS
Slug 48–49
Snail 48–49

MYRIAPODS
Centipede 38–39
Millipede 38–39

WORMS
Earthworm 24–25